First published by Parragon in 2013
Parragon
Chartist House
15–17 Trim Street
Bath BA1 1HA, UK
www.parragon.com

Written by Peter Bently
Edited by Laura Baker
Production by Richard Wheeler
Illustrated by Deborah Melmon
Designed by Ailsa Cullen

ISBN 978-1-4723-2365-1

Printed in China

UNDERPANTS WONDERPANTS

Parragon

Bath • New York • Singapore • Hong Kong • Cologne • Delhi
Melbourne • Amsterdam • Johannesburg • Shenzhen

Is it an eagle?

Is it a plane?

NO – it's **Underpants Wonderpants**

to the **rescue** again!

Whenever you
need him,

in **sun,**
snow
or **shower,**

he'll **sort** out your

problems with

UNDERPANTS POWER!

“Elephant **sat** on our nest!”
grumbles Mouse.

"No problem!"

says **Wonderpants.**

ZAP!

An **underpants** house!

Polar Bear Cub
can't keep up in the **storm.**

ZAP!
Thanks to **Wonderpants** she's **cosy**
and **warm!**

Kangaroo cries,
"I've been **itching** all night!"

ZAP!

In this hammock,
the insects can't **bite**!

The fisherman's ripped a **big** hole in his net. ZAP!

“Thank you, **WONDERPANTS!**
It’s my **biggest** catch yet!”

"Help!" cries the Queen.
It's so far to the ground –

WONDERPANTS' Pantachute helps her land **safe** and **sound!**

Wonderpants zooms to the river,
and in a **great swoop** –

he puts out
the **fire** with his
SUPER-PANT-SCOOP!

But that's not

the **end** of his

super-pants day...

An **alien spaceship** is heading this way!

The **creatures** are
grinning and **shaking**
with **mirth:**
"As soon as we **land**
we'll take over the **Earth!**"

But **imagine** the look on each **alien's** face

when a **WONDERPANTS**

sling sends them – **ZAP!** – back to **space!**

The people all **cheer**

as they **watch** from afar:

"**WONDERPANTS**

saved us all –

"He's our
SUPER-PANTS STAR!"